WELCOME TO
PASSPORT TO READING
A beginning reader's ticket to a brand-new world!

Every book in this program is designed to build read-along and read-alone skills, level by level, through engaging and enriching stories. As the reader turns each page, he or she will become more confident with new vocabulary, sight words, and comprehension.

These PASSPORT TO READING levels will help you choose the perfect book for every reader.

READING TOGETHER
Read short words in simple sentence structures together to begin a reader's journey.

READING OUT LOUD
Encourage developing readers to sound out words in more complex stories with simple vocabulary.

READING INDEPENDENTLY
Newly independent readers gain confidence reading more complex sentences with higher word counts.

READY TO READ MORE
Readers prepare for chapter books with fewer illustrations and longer paragraphs.

This book features sight words from the educator-supported Dolch Sight Words List. This encourages the reader to recognize commonly used vocabulary words, increasing reading speed and fluency.

For more information, please visit passporttoreadingbooks.com.

Enjoy the journey!

Little, Brown and Company

Hachette Book Group
1290 Avenue of the Americas, New York, NY 10104
Visit us at lb-kids.com
mylittlepony.com

Little, Brown and Company is a division of Hachette Book Group, Inc.
The Little, Brown name and logo are trademarks of Hachette Book Group, Inc.

The publisher is not responsible for websites (or their content) that are not
owned by the publisher.

First Edition: January 2017

Library of Congress Control Number: 2016950291

ISBN 978-0-316-27438-8 (paperback);
978-0-316-27437-1 (ebook)

10 9 8 7 6 5 4 3 2 1

CW

Printed in the United States of America

Passport to Reading titles are leveled by independent reviewers applying the standards developed by
Irene Fountas and Gay Su Pinnell in *Matching Books to Readers: Using Leveled Books in Guided Reading*,
Heinemann, 1999.

Licensed By:

Meet Starlight Glimmer

Written by **Magnolia Belle**

LITTLE, BROWN AND COMPANY

New York Boston

Attention, My Little Pony fans!
Look for these words when you read this book.
Can you spot them all?

cutie mark

mess

picnic

relax

Starlight Glimmer is a new
Unicorn in Ponyville.
She learns about magic from
Princess Twilight Sparkle.

Starlight Glimmer loves to learn.
She learns a lot about being
a good friend.

Starlight did not always
want to be a good friend.
She was not nice.

One time, she used magic
to give all ponies
the same cutie mark!

Another time, she tried to stop
Rainbow Dash's Sonic Rainboom.

Twilight saved the day!
She told Starlight about
the Magic of Friendship
and invited her to Ponyville.

Twilight helped Starlight
make new friends with Pinkie Pie,
Rainbow Dash, Fluttershy,
Applejack, and Rarity.

Starlight remembers her old friend Sunburst.
He moved to Canterlot to study magic.

Starlight gets to see Sunburst today!
She is excited, but she is also nervous.

Starlight and Sunburst are both shy.
They do not talk at first.

Starlight uses her magic
to help Sunburst.
They are not shy anymore!

Starlight and Sunburst are
good friends!

Twilight is proud of Starlight
for being a good friend to Sunburst.
Starlight wants to make more friends!

Starlight explores Ponyville
to find a new friend.

First, she bakes cakes
with Pinkie Pie and Mrs. Cake.
Her magic makes a mess.
Mrs. Cake is not happy.

Next, Starlight picks apples
with Applejack and Big Mac.
Her magic scares Big Mac.

Then Starlight visits Rarity.

They play dress-up.

Rarity says dressing up

is a good way to make friends.

Finally, Starlight has a picnic
with Fluttershy.

Starlight has a good day
but is sad she does not
meet new friends.

She visits Ponyville Spa to relax.

She needs to stop worrying.

At the spa,

Starlight meets Trixie.

She is nice!

Trixie once did mean things,
but she wants to be
a good friend now,
just like Starlight.

Starlight is so excited.
She tells Twilight
about her new friend.

Some ponies worry
about Starlight's new friend.
They do not know
Trixie is not mean anymore.

Starlight is a good friend to Trixie.

She says she is a good pony.

The new friends put on a great
magic show together.

Starlight Glimmer is happy
to have a new friend.
They really share the
Magic of Friendship!